THE ADVENTURES OF PIPER THE HYPER MOUSE

Piper's Twisted Tale

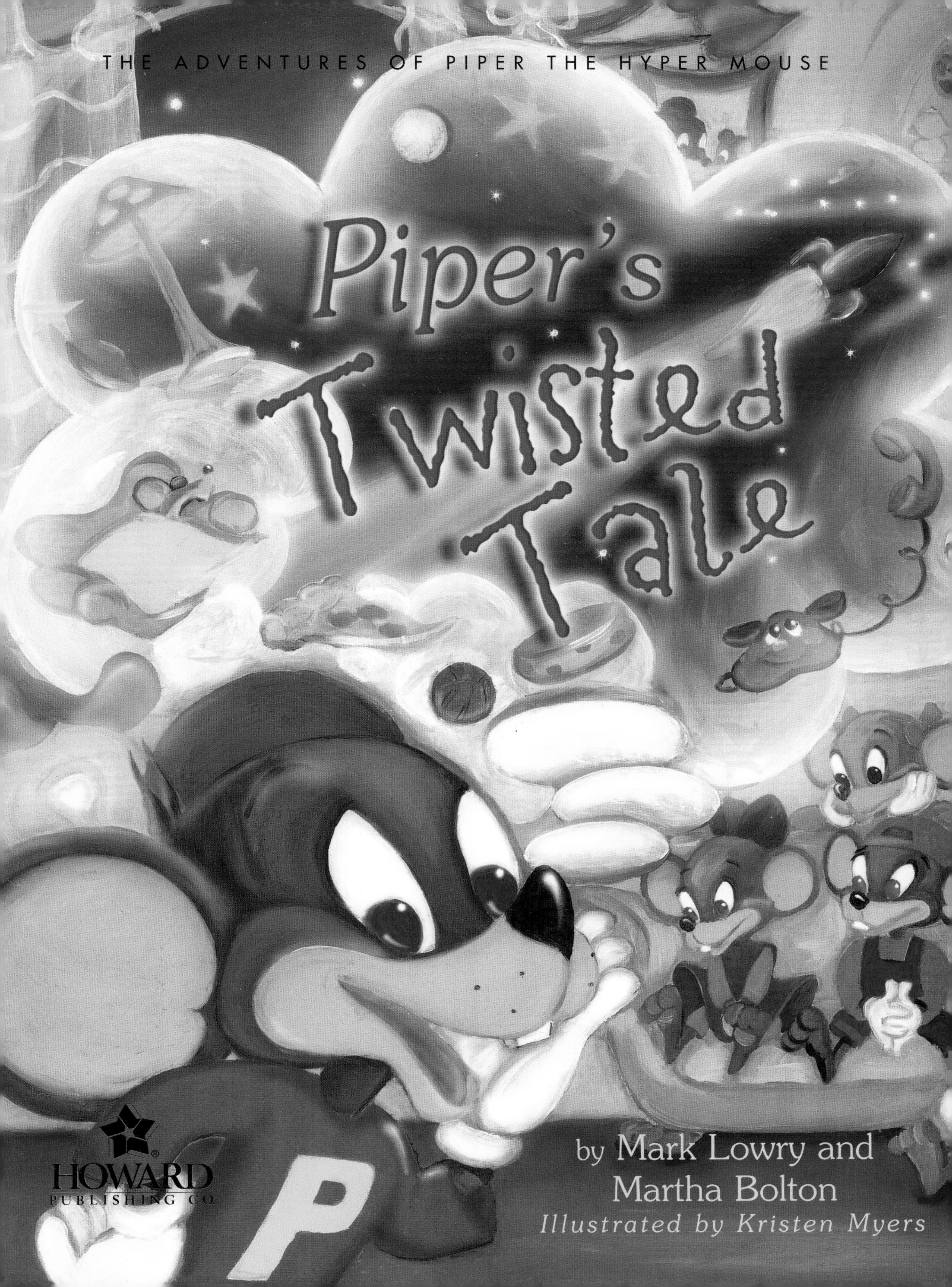

by Mark Lowry and
Martha Bolton
Illustrated by Kristen Myers

HOWARD
PUBLISHING CO.

Our purpose at Howard Publishing is to:

- *Increase faith* in the hearts of growing Christians
- *Inspire holiness* in the lives of believers
- *Instill hope* in the hearts of struggling people everywhere

Because He's coming again!

Piper's Twisted Tale
©2001 Mark Lowry
All rights reserved. Printed in the United States of America

Published by Howard Publishing Co., Inc.,
3117 North 7th Street, West Monroe, Louisiana 71291-2227

01 02 03 04 05 06 07 08 09   10 9 8 7 6 5 4 3 2 1

Illustrated by Kristen Myers
Digital Enhancement by LinDee Loveland

Library of Congress Cataloging-in-Publication Data
Lowry, Mark.
   Piper's twisted tale / Mark Lowry and Martha Bolton ; illustrated by Kristen Myers.
  ISBN 1-58229-192-6

2001039587
CIP

"I'm off to the store,"
Piper's mom said one day.
"You stay right here
And just quietly play."

"Uncle Sylvester
Is taking a nap,
So stay out of trouble
Till I can get back!"

"Mother," said Piper,
"I'll stay in the den
And just watch TV."
And he meant it, but then…

His hyperactivity
Hit like a train!
All sorts of ideas
Popped into his brain!

He called up a friend
And asked if he'd come,
But six mice showed up
By the time he was done!

String Cheese brought pizza.
Cheeseball brought the chips,
And each one took turns
Diving into the dip!

Four quarters of football
And basketball too!

They skied down the stair rails,
Skateboarded the hall.
Poor Uncle Sylvester
Just slept through it all!

They played and they munched.
They munched and they played.
Oh, what a terrible
Mess they all made!

Then all of a sudden
They heard a mouse van
Pull up to the house,
And Piper's friends ran.

They left Piper there
To endure all the shame,
Take all the punishment,
And get all the blame.

Word has it the gasp
Piper's mom gasped that day
Could be heard in the mountains
Two counties away!

"Piper!" she said.
"What on earth happened here?"
She wanted the facts.
That fact was quite clear.

Piper thought for a moment
'Bout all of the fun
He'd had with his friends
And the damage they'd done.

Yet he knew if he told her,
She'd ground him for weeks.
So he made up a story,
But it had a few leaks.

"First came a *tornado*,"
Piper said, "Strangest sight!
It whirled through the house,
Then it called it a night!"

"An earthquake came next,

And an avalanche too!"

"Then two marching bands
Came parading right through!"

Piper spun him a tale
Like no tale you have heard,
And his tail turned and twisted
With every false word.

You see, that's what happens
To mice when they lie.
But Piper ignored it
And simply replied,

"Did I happen to mention
That NASA dropped in
To test a new rocket
Right here in our den?"

"A circus came next,
But what could I say?
Have you ever tried
Shooing lions away?"

While he made up his story—
The wheres, whens, and whats—
Piper's tail kept on twisting
In hundreds of knots.

His mother said, "Son,
That's some tale for a mouse.
Are you sure that all happened
Right here in our house?"

"It really did happen!
It's true," Piper said.
"Thank goodness that I was
Asleep in my bed."

Piper covered his tail
So his mom wouldn't know
That the tale he was spinning,
Well, it wasn't quite so.

"Now, son," she repeated,
"If you're sure that is all,
Then why are there skateboard
Tracks lining the hall?"

"Why did I see your friends
Leaving from here?
And why is there cheese dip
On our chandelier?"

Piper started to sweat,
And he turned a bright red.
If only he'd told her
The whole truth instead.

His tail was in knots!
He was sorry he lied!
But only the truth
Could now get it untied.

Piper knew that confessing
Was what he should do.
And telling the truth was
What God wanted too.

So standing up tall,
Piper laid out the facts
And said he was sorry
For his thoughtless acts.

It took him four days
To clean all the mess,
But he sure felt better
Once he had confessed.

Piper learned that he should have
Obeyed his mom first,
And lying will always
Just make matters worse.

Now Piper can smile,
For inside he feels GREAT!
And his tale and his tail
Are now PERFECTLY STRAIGHT!